PAUL HOPPE (illustrator) has illustrated various children's books, including *Neymar: A Soccer Dream Come True* and *The Woods*, which he also wrote. His work has appeared in publications such as the *New Yorker*, the *Wall Street Journal*, and the *New York Times*. During the summer, Hoppe teaches sequential art at the School of Visual Arts. His work has been honored by the Society of Illustrators, *Communication Arts*, and *American Illustration*, among others. Originally from Poland and raised in Germany, Hoppe works from a shared studio in the Pencil Factory in Brooklyn, and lives in Queens.

"Good Vibrations"
Song written by Mike Love and Brian Wilson
Courtesy of Irving Music, Inc.
Used by Permission. All Rights Reserved.

LyricPop is a children's picture book collection by LyricVerse and Akashic Books.

lyricverse.

Published by Akashic Books
Song lyrics ©1966 Mike Love and Brian Wilson
Illustrations ©2020 Paul Hoppe

ISBN: 978-1-61775-787-7
Library of Congress Control Number: 2019949647
First printing

Printed in Malaysia

Akashic Books
Brooklyn, New York, USA
Ballydehob, Co. Cork, Ireland
Twitter: @AkashicBooks
Facebook: AkashicBooks
E-mail: info@akashicbooks.com
Website: www.akashicbooks.com

GOOD VIBRATIONS

Song lyrics by **Mike Love** and **Brian Wilson**

Illustrations by **Paul Hoppe**

I love the colorful clothes she wears
And the way the sunlight plays upon her hair

I hear the sound of a gentle word

On the wind that lifts her perfume through the air

Good, good, good, good vibrations
She's giving me the excitations

Close my eyes, she's somehow closer now
Softly smile, I know she must be kind

Oh, my my, what

Gotta keep those lovin' good vibrations a-happenin' with her
Gotta keep those lovin' good vibrations a-happenin' with her

Gotta keep those lovin' good vibrations a-happenin' . . .

Do do do do do, do do do